ALONE WITH THE MAID

DIRTY BILLIONAIRE BOSS

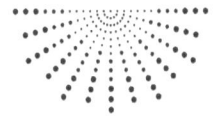

TALA MELTON

plicit Press
Erotica Fiction

GET NAUGHTY UPDATES

Click here or Visit
TalaMelton.com
for more Naughty Maid Stories

eISBN: 978-1-62327-698-0

Print ISBN: 978-1-62327-699-7

CHAPTER ONE

*V*irginia was a far cry from Silicone Valley. *InfiniTechnology*, the multi-billion dollar tech company that had made Raymond Chalmers a billionaire, was rivaled only by *Google* and *Facebook*. He had gotten in the game when software applications were in their infancy, and Raymond had made proverbial hay while the sun was high.

And he wasn't entirely done yet.

He had been working on another deal, one that would forever mark with his name the technology landscape. It would be life-defining, his legacy brought to a spectacular head. But there were details that he still needed to work through, and the devil being in the detail, he was more than a little frustrated. He was actually *a lot* frustrated, and everyone around him was bearing the brunt of this frustration.

"Dinner is ready," Sophie said, peeking through the half-opened study door.

"I said I didn't want to be disturbed," Raymond snapped, before realizing that he was talking to Sophie. The blonde-haired blue-eyed beauty seemed close to tears, having spent the bulk of the afternoon at the receiving end of Raymond's snaps.

"I'm sorry..." Sophie said, and she started to leave, pulling the door shut with her.

"No, no... Come in!" Raymond said, his eyes on the shy girl. "Is everyone still here?" he asked.

"I think so..." Sophie said her voice shakey.

"Tell them all to leave..."

"All of them," she asked.

"What's your name?"

"Sophie, sir..."

"Yes, everyone... Except you, Sophie! And bring my dinner up here..."

* * *

SOPHIE FELT Raymond's eyes on her as she set up the dinner plates on the large study desk. He was watching her with an uncomfortable intensity that made her a little nervous. A few strands of her naturally blonde hair had fallen in her face and stuck to her forehead against the sweat that was forming fast. The salad was cold, but seemed to steam into her face and made her hair stick to her even more.

"Is it too hot in here..." he asked, noticing her sweat.

"No, it's fine," Sophie said, fighting the urge to wipe her brow, struggling to get the tray positioned just right so that she could make her escape.

Raymond sat down behind the desk, turned the air-conditioning down a few degrees. He looked at the three plates in front of him, played with the salad before cutting into the steak. His eyes were still fixed on Sophie, who was now waiting to be released by the billionaire, having just adjusted the third plate for the third time. It contained pieces of fruit.

Her eyes on the floor, she shuffled from foot to foot nervously. She refused to lift her face, scared that her eyes would meet his, not sure what she would be expected to do if this happened. Still, though, she felt his eyes on her, heard him chew. He seemed to be enjoying how uneasy this silence was making her. He seemed to be playing with her, the way a cat might play with its food.

"May I be excused?" she said, at last, clearing her throat.

"Of course... Just pour me drink!" He spoke with such authority that she found herself walking towards the bar despite herself. Her feet seemed to move automatically, one in front of the other, her hands pouring the drink she had never poured in her life before but which she suddenly felt confident enough to pour.

She placed the drink in front of him and paused. He raised two fingers, and she dropped two perfect ice cubes in the glass. Again she paused, waiting for him to release her, waiting to be free from this game she wasn't sure how or when she started playing. She was hotter now despite the lowered temperature, and she just needed to be away from this man who was treating her like she was the only person left in the world.

She was, actually. At least in his world. In this world that was 19-bedrooms and 25 bathrooms, it was just the two of them.

"Do you live on the property?" Raymond asked as he took another tear of the steak from off his stainless steel fork.

"No, sir, I don't..." Sophie was again timid, trying in vain to appear, at least on the surface, more confident than she was.

"Call me Ray, and prepare one of the guest bedrooms for yourself for tonight. I'm going to need you..." She left, at last!

CHAPTER TWO

*S*ophie knew where Raymond's bedroom was, of course, so she took a room on the opposite end of the same floor. This was so that if he needed her, she would be close enough, but also not too close. The discomfort she had felt earlier in the study still lingered.

She closed the door to her bedroom for the night, locking it behind herself. Then, giving it a second thought, she unlocked it. She wasn't sure why, but it just felt wrong somehow to lock a door that wasn't hers.

"It's a little strange..." she said into her phone.

"Strange how?" Her roommate, Carly, really was curious. Carly was a little obsessed with Raymond Chalmers. She read every article on him, kept every published picture of him, and tracked all his movements in mainstream media. She was convinced that the multibillionaire was the inspiration behind *Christian Gray,* so she was beside herself, knowing that Sophie was all alone with the devilishly attractive billionaire.

"I'm not alone with him... I'm just here in case he needs anything..."

"In case he *needs* anything, huh?" Carly really was fishing.

"Oh, shut up!" Sophie said, taking the last of her clothing off. She got onto the large bed in just her panties and finished up what was bordering on an uncomfortable conversation now.

She lay on the bed, thought of how she had felt in Raymond's presence earlier. She had never felt uncomfortable with him before. But then again, she had never been alone with him before, not like this.

Sophie contemplated taking a shower when she remembered that she had left Raymond mid-meal. She thought of the fact too that she hadn't brought a change of clothes with her so that all she had was her uniform and the clothing she had worn to work, jeans and a t-shirt.

Before she knew it, she was under the shower, though. It was quick, incredibly hot, and quite literally the best shower she'd ever had in her life. She slipped into her jeans and tee, and got back on the bed, giving it a minute before she went to get the plates from the study.

Just then, the phone beside her bed was ringing.

"I'm done," was all Raymond said, then he hung up.

She was again caught in a problem, looking at her uniform on the chair. It was a little too short, not her fault, and so again, she made a rather unorthodox decision. She would go in and clear up in her jeans, hiding the parts on her she assumed were the reason for Raymond's stares earlier.

"Have you eaten?" Raymond asked, watching Sophie clear the table.

"No... I'm not a big eater..." she answered without looking up.

"Do you drink?"

"I do..." Sophie answered honestly, not sure why.

"Good... Come back after you're done with this... You can pour *us* a drink!"

She hurried downstairs and walked through the kitchen to the scullery. She loaded all the plates and cutlery in the dishwasher and, in a panic, realized her cellphone was upstairs. Sophie really needed to speak to Carly.

She went into the kitchen, got water from the fridge, and dialed her apartment's landline from the one in the kitchen. The phone seemed to ring forever, and again Sophie was sweating.

"It just got weird..." She said, out of breath.

"First strange, now *weird*... Progress!" Carly could hardly contain her excitement.

"He wants to have a drink with me..."

"Listen, *silly*... He probably just wants to have a drink and a chat with another human being, and you're the only other human being on hand. You said he was stressed. Go have a drink with the man and take his mind off things for a couple of minutes!"

How Carly said '*take his mind off things*' was incredibly loaded. Sophie didn't have the time to think about this now, though, already feeling like she had kept Raymond waiting too long. She hung up the phone without saying goodbye.

"So, what do you do when you're not here?" Raymond asked Sophie as he poured the drinks.

"I'm taking some community college classes...business and law..." she answered, taking the brandy she hadn't said she wanted.

"Smart..." is all Raymond said, his eyes again scanning Sophie so that again she was uncomfortable.

She sipped her drink slowly, unable to avoid his eyes now because they were standing face to face. He looked like he wanted to say something to her like he wanted to ask something of her. But he just kept staring at her until she couldn't take it anymore. Sophie walked to the window overlooking the grounds, saying, "It's beautiful here!"

"It is..." he said, coming up next to her. They both looked out over the many acres, perfectly manicured, lit elegantly by the moon and a few well-placed floodlights.

Raymond finished his drink in a single gulp and watched Sophie nurse hers. "You can do better than that, surely..." he said.

"Just one more," she said, bravely sending the brown liquid down her throat.

It was she who was now watching Raymond as he walked to where the brandy was. He poured two drinks again without asking what Sophie preferred and came back to meet her by the window. He moved like he owned the world. He moved like a god. She couldn't take her eyes off him until he was right next to her again, motioning for them to take a seat on the sofa.

They sat a comfortable distance from each other, chatting easier now. He asked her about her background, seeming genuinely interested. Raymond asked her what things she liked to do, what she enjoyed eating, and where she'd like to travel if she could. She answered him easily, and honestly.

Sophie wanted to know why he was so stressed, what was different about the current project he was working on. He proceeded to explain in detail what she did not understand, which just prompted more questions from a genuinely interested Sophie. The whole setup was starting to feel like a date, almost. It felt like they were getting to know each other.

In a way, they were. Raymond liked to at least know something about the women he slept with.

And he had decided, already, that he was going to sleep with Sophie.

CHAPTER THREE

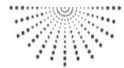

*T*he thought had crossed Sophie's mind, as he chatted, moved closer to her, let his fingers touch the top of her hand mid-sentence. The moment bordered ever so slightly on intimate, and Sophie felt like she was about to turn inside out. She moved her hand away, struggled for something that would get her mind off the man who was now so close to her she could smell him.

"Do I make you uncomfortable?" he asked.

"A little, yes..."

"You're incredibly beautiful..."

Her face flushed red, and she couldn't hide it. Raymond knew exactly what he was doing, a skill perfected through years and years of practice. Seduction was a game he played almost as well as business. He was close to making his intentions clear, but the moment wasn't right, not yet.

He let her finish her drink, allowed her the minute to absorb the compliment before asking her views on casual sex.

"I'm not opposed to the idea..." Sophie's heart was beating incredibly fast now and incredibly loudly.

"And sex in the workplace..." Raymond continued to probe...

"That depends..."

"On?"

"On who in the workplace I'd be sleeping with!" Sophie was surprised by this answer even though it came out of her own mouth.

"The *boss*..." Raymond said as he put his large hand on the back of Sophie's neck and pulled her close enough to kiss her.

It was a passionate kiss, tender and intimate. It was beautiful and heated. She wasn't kissing him back at first, not sure how it had escalated to this so quickly. The conversation had been suggestive, fair enough. It was leading, the direction clear, but not explicit. And now, Raymond was kissing Sophie in a way that let her know that this was just the beginning.

Then Sophie was kissing him back. She played back the whole conversation they had just had as she did. Raymond had asked her everything he needed to. He had made his intentions clear without being demanding about it. He had, in quite a gentlemanly fashion, asked her if she was open to the idea of casual sex with her boss.

He was her boss.

Raymond was on top of her now, positioning her on her back on the sofa. His mouth moved from her lips to her cheek, then her forehead, and then down her neck before finding her mouth again. His hands moved up and down her legs, up and down her back. Her own hands were at her side. She wasn't sure what to do with them yet, not sure if she would let this go any further.

Then his hands were under her t-shirt, and she couldn't breathe. He moved his fingers over her nipples, squeezing her perfect tits, pressing them into her chest before he was again running his fingers over the hard, ripe pods again. Electricity shot through her entire body, which was responding all on its own now. She wrapped her still denim-clad legs around his and kissed him harder, arching her back so that her breasts literally now presented themselves to him.

Raymond unbuttoned his own shirt and took it off before Sophie realized what he was doing. She eyed his chest, soft black curls blanketing the entire surface. Through his curls, she could see his nipples, as ripe and hard as hers. They kissed a moment longer, and then without warning, her own T-shirt was off.

Raymond was a master at what he was doing, and Sophie couldn't help but feel like she was being *conquered*. She was, of course, Raymond doing what it was that alpha male billionaires did.

He was taking what he wanted.

He was being perfectly nice about it, though, which made it easier for Sophie to *let* herself be taken. She hadn't slept with anyone in a while, and if the hard, lengthy shaft rubbing up against her thighs was anything to go by, then sleeping with her billionaire boss was going to prove quite the challenge.

Sophie took a deep breath when Raymond removed his mouth from hers. Then she went for his nipples with her mouth, sucking, then biting. Then she was sucking very hard, and he was groaning. It sounded like she'd imagined it would, despite never having thought before that she would ever be in this position with this particular man. It really was strange and weird, and a whole lot of other things that she could not articulate.

Then they were turned so that Sophie was sitting on top of him. She didn't know what or how he was doing what he was, but the control he exhibited was incredible. She felt like she was a puppet on very beautiful strings that only

Raymond knew how to pull. It was incredibly easy to surrender to a man who knew exactly where he was leading you.

His hands felt for her jeans button and undid it. Then his hand slipped down the front of her over her panties and made the slightest contact with *ground zero*. Again she felt shards of electricity going through her, up her belly and through her breasts before making their way up the back of her neck and over her head.

She thought of unbuttoning his trousers too but was still a little nervous. She wasn't sure, in fact, if this would go any further, even though Raymond's finger was now pressing against all the *technical* parts of her femininity. Again, Sophie couldn't breathe, and Raymond relished the fact that it was he who rendered her breathless.

"Are you okay with this?" he asked after he kissed her again.

She wasn't sure. She really wasn't. But she had to give him an indication either way. With the wheels turning in her head visible on her face, Raymond stopped what he was doing. He had to be sure that she was sure.

Sophie came down onto his chest, taking his nipples into her mouth again. She sucked hard and then bit harder as she used both her hands on his button and then his zip. He smiled and slipped his finger underneath her panties, making direct contact with her for the first time. He used his other hand to pull his pants down enough to expose what really was a very big *problem*.

She took another long breath, pushed herself against his finger, and leaned down, so their lips met. She was trembling now, and again Raymond was excited that he was the cause. It had been a while since a woman responded to him this way, and it was doing all sorts of things to his ego.

Again they moved, Raymond on top of her now, pulling

her jeans off completely, not leaving her panties behind. He took his own trousers off so that finally, they were both completely naked...

CHAPTER FOUR

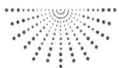

*H*e took her legs in his hands, separated them. He planted his face between her thighs and sucked hard. Again Sophie felt like she was about to turn inside out. She felt like everything inside her was being sucked out of the place where his mouth attached itself to her.

Then Raymond wasn't sucking. He was licking her, *all of her*, pressing the entire surface of his tongue on every part of her that mattered. It was hard for Sophie to distinguish between the sucking and the licking, to say definitively, which was more intense. And just as she was settling into this sensation, he was using just the tip of his tongue on her engorged lips.

This flicking lasted an eternity too. She heard him, mid-lick, mumble something, but she didn't care what he was saying. She held on to his head to brace herself, which strange because *she was literally holding on to the reason she needed to brace herself in the first place*. She laughed at this thought, and Raymond stopped what he was doing, looked up at her.

"It's nothing," she said, pushing his face down on her

again.

He decided to let it go. Sophie tasted incredible, so to interrupt this *feast* in favor of conversation made absolutely no sense to him.

His tongue was working on her again, more intentionally this time, it seemed. It seemed to have found a rhythm almost and was determined not to skip a beat. The melody was magnificent.

"You taste amazing," he said when he could pull his mouth off her.

"Thank you," is all she could manage.

Then his whole mouth was back on her, creating a perfect seal, and sucking so hard that she thought she was having an orgasm. It couldn't be, though. Sophie knew what an orgasm felt like. She knew that this wasn't it.

Or maybe it was. Maybe for the first time in her life, she has experienced a genuine climax. If this was the case, then everything she'd thought about sex was wrong. Even the way she'd touched herself was wrong.

"Oh my god..." she said, over and over again. She couldn't breathe so that she could hear these words coming out of her mouth surprised her.

"Just relax and enjoy it," is all Raymond said, bringing her closer and closer to the orgasm she wasn't quite having yet, but which she was convinced that she was.

His tongue went inside her now, deep inside her. She flowed just that much more, wrapped her legs tighter around his neck. His tongue darted deep inside her and then all the way out. In again, completely, and then all the way out. Over and over again, she was pierced by this fleshy organ that was melting her from the inside, all the heat from his mouth transferring into her depths on each insertion.

It was almost surgical in its precision. Military was another word that came to mind. Still, Sophie hadn't cum, but she was incredibly close. She just had no idea what to do with these incredible sensations, literally firing all over her body.

And then it happened.

Her legs fell into a spread eagle, pushed down at the thighs by Raymond's firm grip. He pushed down hard and went in deeper with his tongue. He pushed hard against *everything* inside Sophie that now just needed an out. And it was coming out hard, directly into Ray's mouth.

Sophie was gasping. She wanted to scream, knew that she could, but didn't. She had never ever *ever* experienced such an epic *end* in her entire life. She couldn't move. She was shaking, but couldn't move of her own free will. The parts of her brain that linked to her body were broken; or temporarily out of service.

Raymond licked her tenderly now. And then he was kissing the skin around her navel, and then almost *French Kissing* her belly-button. His mouth found her nipples; Sophie was still incapable of voluntary movements. He sucked hard, and then he was just kissing the surface of her breasts. Then his mouth was on her neck, then her mouth again.

Her legs started to move now, the movement directed by her brain, sort of. She tried to wrap her legs around his legs, but still, she couldn't follow through with this instruction completely.

Then Raymond was looking at her, directly at her. Her eyes were opened too, and she was looking at him. He said nothing, pressing her into the sofa with his weight. He moved in small incremental movements, positioning his thickness over her tender volcano that, just seconds earlier, had been erupting. She knew that she had no way of resisting him if she changed her mind. She also knew that she would not resist him at all right now; she just couldn't!

Raymond started to ease himself into her. He went slowly, savoring every moment. He also knew that his thickness and length meant that he had to proceed with extreme caution right now. He eased himself into her until he was a quarter of the way in. Then he thrust, slow and sensual, with just the parts of him already inside her.

Then he got halfway in. Again his thrusts were slow, deliberate. There was just something so incredibly controlled with what he was doing to her that again she surrendered easily. For the briefest moment, she questioned whether this was a good idea, and then she dismissed the question without answering it.

Raymond didn't try for any more. He didn't need to. He just knew that he was bringing her closer and closer to a second climax. Her eyes were closed again, and he was looking at her pretty face. She was present with him in every way possible, in every way that mattered, so that it didn't bother him that she wasn't looking at him.

In fact, this excited him even more...

With slow, determined strokes, he brought Sophie to yet another orgasm. This one was even more intense than the first, which she wasn't expecting. She didn't think it was possible, in fact, a part of her waiting for him to climax instead.

He didn't!

"Don't you need to...finish?" She asked him this once she had reoriented herself and only after Raymond had exited her.

"No, I don't! This was all about you..." Again this sounded date-like, but Sophie wasn't about to interrogate it.

"What about you?" She was really wondering.

He just looked down at her, smiled, and got up to pour them both a drink.

CHAPTER FIVE

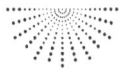

*A*fter the drink, Sophie gathered her clothing and went to her bedroom. Raymond was terribly civilized, no longer strange, no longer weird. He kissed her on her cheek and whispered, "*thank you...*" in her ear. He left her outside her door.

What had just happened was all Sophie could think, under another piping hot shower. The jets coming down at her and on from every possible angle were rivaled only by what Raymond had just done to her. It really was something spectacular. He seemed different after, in a good way. He appeared energized, ready to conquer the world. He liked that he had brought her to her knees, and she was happy that she had given him a second wind.

She wondered as she lathered herself, if he would work, or if he would have another drink and reminisce. Fortunately, Sophie wasn't the type to catch feelings, regardless, and she went into this with eyes wide open. So, relaxing into the beauty of the moment, she just enjoyed the shower.

She wrapped herself in one of the luxurious towels that were aplenty in the bathroom. Rich folk really did everything in excess, she thought. Sophie walked out onto the balcony and took in the almost 1 AM air. The chill was bearable, typical of a Virginia autumn.

Sophie wondered if she should call Carly. Would she be awake, waiting by the phone for her to *give up all* the glorious details? She decided that she'd let her stew a little. One night won't kill her.

Meanwhile, one floor down in the study, Raymond was also standing outside, still naked. The chill against his bare chest was just what he needed. He really did feel better. You didn't know what you needed until it showed up, and what Raymond really needed tonight was Sophie.

He went back inside and had a quick shower in the bathroom, just off the study. He wrapped himself in one of his towels and set about piecing together the problem that had him on edge for the last couple of weeks. He didn't solve the complex problem in one fell swoop, a single swift stroke of his mighty sword, but he did make significant enough progress, the progress that he knew would not have been possible had he not just been inside Sophie.

When he was done for the night, it was almost 5 AM. With work done, he could now focus on his own climax, abandoned earlier in order to give Sophie two. He wondered if she was awake. He wondered if she'd mind. He was wondering a lot of things, and so he just poured himself another drink. He really did drink a lot.

Sophie was half asleep, half not. She, too, had spent most of the night hoping that Raymond would slip into her room to finish what he started, if not for her, then at least for himself. He didn't come though, and she had fallen into a light half-sleep just after 3:30.

He tried her door handle gently, not wanting to wake her in case the door was locked. That would be embarrassing, him standing outside her door in nothing but a towel, *coming for some more.* Raymond knew though, somehow, that she wouldn't think that. They had both enjoyed the tryst, immensely.

The door opened easily. Raymond breathed a sigh of relief. He pushed the door open and stepped into the still-dark room. He made out the *pile of person* in the bed, but he wasn't sure if she was awake. He would just walk in, go up to the bed if she was awake, then she was. If she wasn't, then that would just be that.

She sat up in bed, and Raymond stopped moving. She knew it could only be him, but her eyes were still adjusting to the light. There was a moment of silence, and a long awkward silence made more awkward by the semi-darkness.

"Are you awake," he asked, feeling *discovered.*

"I've been up for a while," she said, her eyes still struggling to adjust.

Raymond could obviously see very well in the dark because she had hardly finished her sentence, and he was on the bed. He found her lips with his own, pulling the towel from around him and throwing it on the floor. She was already naked, which he liked. *She had been expecting him.*

"You inspired me," he whispered, pulling the duvet off her because it was forming a makeshift barrier between them.

"I'm glad," she said, positioning herself underneath him so that he again had access to her.

Raymond kissed her passionately, turning her over so that she was now lying on her stomach. His mouth never left hers once, even with his morning *wood* grinding against her butt-cheeks. It was thicker, somehow—more threatening. And Sophie wasn't ready for him to park his pecker *there*.

She had nothing to worry about, though. Raymond was not about to put himself where she wasn't ready, and if his experience had taught him one thing, it was that women were very seldom ready to be *rear-ended* so early in the morning.

Most women, anyway...

He was kissing her up and down her back now. Then his lips found the firmness of her butt-cheeks. He kissed them over and over again before he was working his way up to her neck again. He parted her legs, just a little.

Sophie raised herself at the hips so that he had easier access to her. She wanted him to take his time, but she also wanted him in her, all the way. She wanted to experience the fullness of him before this was over. When she left the house, it could be today, could be tomorrow, but when she left, she knew that this might never happen again. And so she wanted to milk the experience.

Raymond was having the same thoughts. He wondered as he teased her with the possibility of himself if an opportunity like this would present itself after the weekend. He was accustomed to getting his own way, and so he knew that he could probably have her again if he wanted to. He would just need to make sure that she was left wanting now.

His concerns were just as unfounded as hers. Raymond represented for Sophie everything she wanted, physically, in a man. For him, she was everything that a woman should be, and a whole lot more. Neither of them would articulate their concerns to each other; there was no need. They were here, together, now, and that's all that mattered.

Raymond was sliding himself up and down between her thighs, still just threatening, her head tilted back slightly so that his lips could find hers again.

There was nothing to say now, between them, the billionaire about to take, for the first time really, Sophie, *completely*.

He parted her legs with a side to side movement of his waist, and then he was inside her, just his head, too quickly. She spread her legs a little more, not wanting him to struggle, not wanting anything about this situation to stop *because* of her. Raymond eased the first few inches of himself in her, and she took it like a champ.

He was thrusting now, measured, calculated. He was in no hurry; neither was she. He put himself higher up on the bed so that his hands gripped the wrought iron headboard. Then he tried, still measured, for a little more of Sophie. She gave it up easily. With half his thick throbbing tentpole inside her, he stopped. He looked at her face, her eyes open now.

"Are you okay?"

"I'm good," she said.

This wasn't a lie, too. Raymond could have had anyone of her many crevices, and she would have let him. There was nothing that he asked for that he couldn't have. This wasn't even because he was her boss or a billionaire. It was just because he was such a gentleman, *painfully polite* about pleasing her.

He kissed her mouth as he started to move. It was wonderful how aware he was of himself; this awareness obviously in the way he *took care* of her. This must be the allure of the older man, Sophie thought. Experience and practice made them extremely capable lovers.

Raymond was certainly capable.

He knew what he wanted, how to ask for it, and how to take it when it was willing. This, Sophie thought, must be just one of the reasons for his enormous success. Her head was really spinning with thoughts of *Ray* beyond what he was now doing to her and with her. These thoughts were arrested, though, when unexpectedly, two more thick inches made their way into her.

She moaned.

Raymond loved it, feeding her a further inch, drawing another moan from her.

Then he was digging into her with just the parts of him she had already accepted. It was all he needed for now. It was all she could take for now. So, for now, they milked this connection for everything it was worth.

Sophie suddenly secreted enough of her sensual syrup to take every last inch of Raymond into her. This was unexpected, for both of them; the orgasm Sophia was having really crept up on her, caught her completely by surprise. Ray stopped moving completely and looked down at her. She had her eyes closed now, but her mouth completely open.

No sound was coming from her, though.

There was no movement for another long minute. Sophie reassured Ray with her eyes that she really was okay. He wasn't so sure and started to pull out slowly.

"No..." she said.

"Are you sure," he asked.

"Completely... Absolutely!"

He settled back inside her and moved from side to side, an effort to stretch her just a little more. Then he was pulling almost all the way out and going all the way in with the greatest care.

CHAPTER SIX

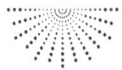

*T*he fit was still incredibly tight, but manageable. So much so that Ray felt comfortable enough to turn them over, albeit carefully, so that he was now on his back, Sophie joined to him at the waist. She wasn't as ready for this as she thought she was, as he thought she was, though, and so she placed her hands on Raymond's chest, lifted herself ever so slightly off him.

He lay back and placed his hands on her thighs, not moving her in any way now. He just let her do what she needed, what she wanted, what she could. Sophie settled down on him again, again taking every last inch of him into her. She was braced, her hands on his chest still. Slowly, too slowly almost, Sophie lifted herself off him, until he was half in half out. And then she eased herself down on him until every inch of him was again inside her.

She let her hands move down on his chest, to his stomach, so that she was really straddling him now. More of him seemed to be inside her, and she stopped moving. Before Ray had a chance to process this pause, though, she was moving again, small sensual circles that sent the same electricity he had transferred to her but a few hours earlier.

His hands had moved onto her waist now, and now he was moving her. She was really a champion, but if he was going to meet his orgasm face to face, he would have to assume some of the control back. Raymond thought that he could hold out, let her enjoy herself, let her acclimatize, but he saw his own climax now, like a vehicle in his rearview mirror, and he was intent on not letting it pass him by. There would be time for relaxed play later, he knew.

Up and down, all the way up and all the way down, he was moving her. She lifted her hands off his belly now and put her hands behind her, on his legs. Using this necessary leverage, Sophie moved herself in wider circles on him, allowing him the control of the up and down. Then it was Raymond who was moving her in circles, Sophie raising and lowering herself on his hardness.

"Why have we never done this before," he asked, not to her directly.

She couldn't answer him. Not right now. All her focus had to be on what was going on between her legs. Sophie was really grinding against him now, arresting control from him once more. This wasn't intentional. But there were places inside her that Ray just *missed*, both on the up-down and the circular.

There was a strange disconnect between them now, and it took them a minute to realize why. Raymond was close, Sophie was close, and they were both concentrating on getting the other one over to the *Land of Milk and Honey*.

Someone needed to surrender. Someone needed to give, or else both of them would miss this opportunity. Words couldn't come out of Sophie's mouth, though. And Ray, for all the control and command he had of himself and the situation, was struggling to form coherent sentences in his head.

One thing stood in his favor. He was an *alpha*. He was a *beast*. And now, more than ever was the time he needed to what it was that beasts did. Raymond gripped her hips, hard, pushed her down on him as he thrust as hard, up and into her. She stopped moving.

He pulled her towards him, dragging on his hardness in the same direction as his still solid erection. Then he pushed her hand away from him, dragging his erection in the opposite direction.

The drag was incredible, the sensation intense. Sophie let out a moan so loud it bordered on a scream. Raymond grunted, loud and continuous so that it sounded like the primal mating calls of an Amazonian beast. The sounds almost echoed in the room now spectacularly lit by dawn.

The push and pull was all Raymond needed. It was the only movement required for him to cross over. It was all she needed because she was in the throes of climax. She was still screaming, despite her best efforts not to. Ray just pushed and pulled her harder, milking her for everything she had left in her.

Now, it was his turn. He had to remain focused now. Sophie was spent; he knew this. So he knew she couldn't last too much longer with his exaggerated proportions inside her, not in any way that would still be comfortable for her, at least.

Raymond pushed her down on him, turned himself so that he was again on top of her. He was already thrusting before she was flat on her back. When she was, he was hitting it so hard that she felt the mattress would give. She couldn't move her legs again but felt them part at Ray's grip.

He hammered her hard, all the way in, naval deep, over and over and over again. He was incredibly close. He felt this in every part of him. He just needed her to hold on just a moment longer. Just a little while longer.

"Almost," he whispered.

He gave her several swift strokes before again whispering, "*Almost!*"

He said *almost* with each subsequent stroke, hitting the depths of her hard, a second's pause at the end of each stroke so that Sophie too was now convinced that he was close.

When Sophie thought she couldn't anymore, just as she was about to utter the words she was determined not to, it happened. Raymond was suddenly deathly quiet. She didn't hear a sound coming from him, but she felt his climax, warm and excessive inside her. It filled her up to her breasts, a tingle moving swiftly over the nape of her neck and over her head, flushing her face crimson.

Raymond had stopped moving completely now, a dead weight on top of her. She could feel him breathing, but still, he said nothing. He couldn't. He could barely think. This was, for them both, the most spectacular sex they had had in quite a while.

"Wow..." Raymond said at last.

Sophie still found words difficult, and she just lay there and let him lift himself up and out of her.

CHAPTER SEVEN

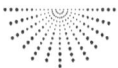

*S*ophie woke up just afternoon. She was alone in the bed, no idea when Raymond had left. In fact, she couldn't remember the last thing either of them had said before she passed out.

Or maybe he had passed out first?

She didn't know...

After a long, necessary shower, she made the bed up with fresh sheets, taking the dirty linens to the washing machine. She hoped not to bump into Raymond, not sure what his thoughts were about what had happened between them. She put on a fresh pot of coffee, and sat in the kitchen courtyard, taking in the chill. The day was colder than the night had been, a sure sign that winter was close.

"Did you sleep okay," he asked, standing in the kitchen door, coffee in hand.

"I did... I don't remember..." she started...

"Don't worry, neither do I... I think I was really drunk..."

"I wasn't!"

They both laughed, not sure at what, though.

Raymond came out to her and sat down opposite her. He

looked at her in her face, in her eyes, the way he had looked at her last night when she thought he wanted to ask her something.

"Do we have to have a conversation..." he asked.

"No... We're two consenting adults... So as long as my job isn't affected, there is nothing to say!"

"Good... And no... Not at all!"

They chatted easily now, the elephant in the room that wasn't really an elephant sufficiently addressed.

* * *

"NOTHING HAPPENED," she lied to Carly.

"I know you..." Carly said, dragging her roommate into their apartment, sitting her down in a high wingback they had purchased at a thrift store and looked her square in her face. Sophie wondered why people were so comfortable staring her square in the face.

She couldn't lie. Her own face betrayed her so that barely five minutes since her arrival home to *collect a change of clothing,* she was revealing to *Curious* Carly every detail of the naughty night she spent with her *dirty* billionaire boss.

Carly savored every word. She hung like a hungry child on a fruit tree to every delicious syllable that fell from Sophie's lips. It was everything she'd imagined it would be and then some. The pangs of jealousy were tempered only by the fact that it had happened to her friend.

"So, you're going back," Carly asked.

"That's the plan!"

"To be on hand in case he needs you?"

"That's the idea..."

"Do you think he will... Need you?"

"*Oh god, I hope so*

ABOUT THE AUTHOR

Tala Melton is an emerging erotica author of naughty maids and their billionaire bosses.

Readers: I want to expand a few of the stories to see where the characters can be explored further. If there are any of the stories that you would like to read more about again, I'd love to hear from you!

Visit my blog at Tala Melton Blog
Join my newsletter for free exclusive previews Tala Melton Newsletter
Follow me on Twitter at Tala Melton Twitter
Like my page on Facebook at Tala Melton FB

Sign up for Free Stories from Xplicit Press Authors
Xplicit Press Updates
Like Xplicit Press on Facebook
Follow Xplicit Press on Twitter

MORE NAUGHTY MAID STORIES BY TALA MELTON